This book belongs to ______________________________

A purple umbrella for my niece, Ellie.

Little Oak Publishing
London, UK
This edition published in Great Britain 2024

Character illustrations by Elena Sosnina

ISBN 978-1-7399500-8-8

@franpicturebooks

Sophie the Sunflower

Little Oak Publishing

Sophie was dancing with excitement under the fresh rain which made her grow. The raindrops made her shine so brightly that sometimes they sparkled like stars on her petals.

Sophie loved growing alone in the meadows. It was a peaceful place that always made her happy. It was morning, and she was having the bubbliest time at home.

‘POP!’ giggled Sophie.

But as the sun wrapped her in a cosy warm hug, her stem felt strangely slimy! 'Hello, I'm Sam, your new neighbour,' said the slug. 'Yum! What a tasty stem!'

'I'm not a snack. Go away!' grumbled Sophie.

But there were just many things that Sam loved about Sophie. ‘It’s so comfy here, and your petals smell delightful! I could live here forever!’ said Sam, happy to have found a new home.Until...

A gigantic shadow loomed over them, and Sophie's roots ripped from the earth and soared into the sky. 'Ooouucchh!' shouted Sophie.'Wwweee! I'm flying like a bird!' laughed Sam.

Sophie and Sam travelled across the forest and rivers far from home only to find themselves in a big

SPLASH!

‘We better close our eyes for the ride!’ said Sam, as the wild current pushed them down. Down and down, they went, spinning, flipping and twirling until...

It felt like the world stood still! 'How are we going to get out of here?' wondered Sophie.

When suddenly, an idea popped into her head.

Sophie spread her petals widely and tilted her head towards the sky. With a cheerful captain on board, she floated like a boat.

'We're the pirates of the sea!' giggled Sam.

'Hooray! We made it!' said Sam. But Sophie shivered. 'That was the worst! I'll never touch a drop of water again!' she sighed.

‘We’re lost in an unknown forest,’ said Sophie, sadly. Sam happily crawled around the ground checking out their new surroundings.

Sophie did her best to keep dry.

Then, she found a nice place to rest. 'Ah, perfect!' she thought as she drifted off with a snore.

But, ***crunch***!
'What a delicious lunch!' said Sam, chomping on Sophie's bed.

Without water for so long, Sophie stopped growing. She was withered and limp. 'I'm worried about you,' said Sam, kindly offering a fresh cup of water. 'Yuk!' said Sophie.

And for the very first time, Sophie shared her sorrows with a friend. ‘What if I never grow again? I miss the meadows so much,’ sobbed Sophie. Streams of tears trickled down her cheeks.

In the middle of Sophie's worry, Sam kindly lent an ear to her sorrows. When suddenly, Sophie's roots strangely started to...

Tickle!

'Sam, is that you?' said Sophie.
'Who, me? I'm just surfing on waves of fun!' laughed Sam.

Then, suddenly, the world seemed a little smaller beneath Sophie's eyes. 'Whoooaaa! I'm taller than fungi,' said Sophie. Her tears had made her grow and her petals gleamed like the sun.

'Maybe, we can make our way back now, but how?' said Sophie, lost in wonder again. Sam scanned the woods, when a light bulb moment struck.'I know! If we follow the slime trails on the trees, I think we can get home before dark.'

Sam yawned as his eyes grew bigger out of tiredness.'We can do this, Sam,' said Sophie, wrapping her favourite leaf around him. And with each slimy stride, slowly, they headed towards the meadows.

'Sam, we're home!' said Sophie, whose smile briefly turned into a frown as the rain began to sprinkle from the sky. But she knew she needed water to grow, and with a friend by her side, she felt a little better.

The meadow was livelier now, and that evening, Sophie grew brighter than ever before. Under the twinkling stars, Sophie and Sam told each other stories until...

Sam fell asleep.
Then, Sophie too soundly fell into a deep slumber.

About Sophie the Sunflower

Dear readers,

I hope this book evokes conversations with children about the importance of evolving friendships and emotional release through self-expression.
In this story, Sophie is initially growing in the meadows with no one by her side. This metaphor relates to a possible lack of emotional support by our surroundings. Talking to someone about our sorrows helps us process and understand our feelings better. Whilst there are many ways of processing sadness, this story especially embraces the value of connection between friends and the people around us. Sharing our thoughts and sadness with another can increase self-awareness, self-expression, emotional resilience, empathy, hope, self-acceptance, and reduce loneliness, fear and helplessness.

With love,

Françoise Hélène

About the Author

Françoise Hélène is an award-winning Poet and Author. In her poetry, she writes about the relationships between nature, the arts, music and health. She also writes children's picture books to enhance understanding of children's emotional and social development, alongside bedtime meditations to help enrich children's wellbeing. She's a qualified researcher who specialises in literature and wellbeing and an early-year's teacher. Occasionally, she writes song lyrics and has a particular fondness for singing in French, being her first language.

If you enjoyed reading this book, an online review would be immensely appreciated.

Little Oak Publishing

@FRANPICTUREBOOKS

Milton Keynes UK
Ingram Content Group UK Ltd.
UKRC031313120924
448173UK00024B/68

* 9 7 8 1 7 3 9 9 5 0 0 8 8 *